D0880723

The Wounded Duck

Text copyright © 1979 Peter Barnhart / Illustrations copyright © 1979 Adrienne Adams / Copyright under the Berne Convention
All rights reserved / Printed in the United States of America
Library of Congress Catalog Card Number 79-88022 / SBN 0-684-16255-5
1 3 5 7 9 11 13 15 17 19   RD/C   20 18 16 14 12 10 8 6 4 2

The Wounded Duck

by Peter Barnhart

illustrated by Adrienne Adams

Charles Scribner's Sons • New York

"My bones weren't made for this weather," said the old woman one December morning, as she fed the duck a handful of corn. Her chest ached and her breathing was heavy.

"I'm going south for the winter. But don't you worry. Tomorrow you're going to the neighbor's farm, where there's plenty to eat and a pen to keep you safe and warm at night."

She went inside to pack her clothes and put her tiny house in order.

That evening she sat by the fire and remembered the many winters she and the duck had spent together. The thought of leaving made her sad, but her body was withered and weak, not fit for another season of ice and snow.

Later that night there was a bitter wind and the first snow began to fall. In the middle of her sleep the old woman was awakened by a fierce squawking and the sound of flapping wings, coming from the pond. She threw on her shawl, took a flashlight from the cupboard and headed into the storm to find the duck.

"Lord love a duck!" she whispered. "The coons have got you this time." There on the ice lay the duck, his neck outstretched and his eyelids torn and scratched. There was blood on the claws of his webbed feet. In the snow around him there wasn't a sign of footprints, but the old woman didn't notice. She wrapped the duck in her shawl and carried him inside for the night.

She put wood on the fire and sat with the duck in her lap, singing softly to herself.

"Oh, the lord loves the duck,
And the duck loves me.
Our souls will rest,
'Neath the wide willow tree."

"Quack-quack!" went the duck. "Quack-quack!" And the old woman knew he would survive.

She swabbed his face with a warm, damp cloth. His eyes opened. Then she lit a match and passed it in front of his beak. But his head didn't turn and his eyes didn't follow the flame.

"Well," said the old woman, "going south is a nice idea, but I couldn't very well leave a blind duck with the neighbor, now could I?"

The next morning the ache in her chest had disappeared and her breathing was lighter. She began teaching the duck to come to the sound of her voice.

Before winter was over, he could go straight to her hand from anywhere on the pond, even if it meant slipping and sliding over the ice. All the old woman had to say was, "Quack-quack!"

Spring passed into summer and summer into fall. When the leaves fell and the nights grew chilly, the old woman felt a familiar ache in her hands and feet and a strange numbness in her left side.

"My bones weren't made for this weather," she said one windy morning, as she fed the duck. Her left hand shook and the corn fell to the ground. "I'm going south for the winter. But don't you worry. Tomorrow you're going to the neighbor's farm, where there's plenty to eat and a pen to keep you safe and warm at night."

That evening there was a full moon. Coyotes
howled in the nearby woods. As she dozed in her rocking chair, the old woman was awakened by a squawk,
a splash and a flap-flap-flap! She wrapped a blanket
around her shoulders and trudged out to the pond in
the moonlight.

There in the water at the foot of the weeping willow tree, lay the duck. As the old woman drew near, she saw that the sides of his head were scratched and bloody. A patch of his feathers was stuck to the tree, but she paid no attention.

"Lord love a duck!" she whispered, "the coyotes have got you this time."

She wrapped him in the blanket and went inside.

All night they sat by the fire and the old woman talked softly to herself in words that meant nothing at all. By morning the duck lifted his head and opened his beak. "Quack-quack!" A smile appeared on the woman's face. She felt the duck's warmth against her chest and fell asleep.

When the sun had warmed the air, she awoke and carried the duck outside to the shore of the pond.

"You must be as weak as a kitten. Wait while I fetch you some food."

"Quack-quack!" she called, reaching out with a handful of corn. "Quack-quack!" But the duck didn't move. "Quack-quack!" she shouted, bending low, but the duck seemed not to hear.

"I might as well quack at the moon," she said to herself. "The poor thing is deaf."

She passed the corn back and forth in front of his nostrils. His head followed her hand, getting closer and closer, until his beak touched the corn and he ate.

"You've lost your eyes and ears, but your sniffer's as good as ever. You'll have to learn to follow your nose. That's all there is to it. And I'll have to give up my fancy ideas about going south. I couldn't very well leave a blind, deaf duck with the neighbor, now could I?"

The old woman raised her left hand and looked at her knobby fingers. The trembling of the day before had gone. She barely noticed the numbness in her side.

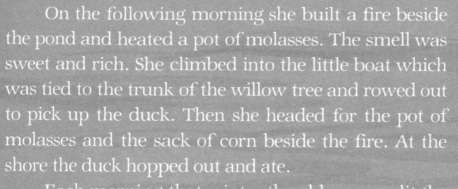

On the following morning she built a fire beside
the pond and heated a pot of molasses. The smell was
sweet and rich. She climbed into the little boat which
was tied to the trunk of the willow tree and rowed out
to pick up the duck. Then she headed for the pot of
molasses and the sack of corn beside the fire. At the
shore the duck hopped out and ate.

Each morning that winter the old woman lit the
fire beside the pond. The duck smelled the molasses
and paddled over to get his corn.

"Quack-quack!" he said, when his gullet was full.
"Quack-quack!"

The old woman watched from the kitchen window and sang softly to herself.

"Oh, the lord loves the duck,
And the duck loves me.
Our souls will rest,
'Neath the wide willow tree."

The duck's sense of smell seemed to improve as winter passed. By summer he could find his food anywhere on shore, molasses or not.

Then fall arrived with a gust of wind from the north. The old woman shivered. Her body knew it had seen enough winters and was ready for a long, long rest.

"My bones weren't made to last forever," she said one drizzly morning, as she opened the sack of corn for the duck. Her knees and hips were stiff. The old woman sat down to rest on a rock beside the pond.

The duck picked at the large yellow kernels in the sack, then laid his head in the palm of her hand.

That night she carried him inside and they sat by the hearth in her rocking chair.

"You aren't going to get yourself wounded again," she said. "You're staying inside, where it's safe and warm."

She coughed and her thin body quivered. Her lungs felt as if they were filled with the dampness and cold of many winters.

"I won't be here come spring, that's for sure," and she patted the soft, smooth down on the duck's back. "But don't you worry. You'll be going to the neighbor's farm, where there's plenty to eat and a pen to keep you safe and warm at night."

Suddenly there was a dizzy feeling in her head and her heart jumped, like a bird taking flight. Her eyes closed. She leaned back in the rocker and began singing softly to herself.

"Oh, the lord loves the duck,
And the duck loves…"

The words stopped and so did the beating of her heart. A smile appeared upon her lips and she went to sleep. It was the sleep of great peace that lasts forever.

The next day the neighbor came by and found the old woman with the duck in her lap. The fire had burned itself down to a few glowing cinders.

That afternoon the old woman was buried at the foot of the wide willow tree.

The neighbor carried the duck back to his farm and put him in a pen with food and straw and a fence outside to keep away the wild animals at night. But the duck didn't eat or sit in the straw. Instead, he waddled the length of the chicken wire fence, tapping it with his beak.

After sniffing the air in all directions, he flapped his powerful wings, pushed the earth with his strong webbed feet and flew.

Over the fence he went and across the field. He smelled the pond and the willow tree and came to light on the old woman's grave.

"Quack-quack!" he said.
"Quack-quack!" Then he
settled down with his
head beneath his wing and went
to sleep.

Title: The Wauncled Duck

Author: peter Barnhart

Out	Name	In

LOVE